Daisy Fleabane

The Library of Congress has cataloged the Lothrop, Lee & Shepard Books edition of *Counting Wildflowers* as follows: McMillan, Bruce. Counting wildflowers. Summary: A counting book with photographs of wildflowers illustrating the numbers one through twenty. 1. Counting—Juvenile literature. 2. Wild Flowers—Juvenile literature. [1. Wild flowers. 2. Counting] I. Title ▪ QA113.M4 ▪ 1986 ▪ 513'.2 [E] ▪ 85-16607 ▪ ISBN 0-688-02859-4 ▪ ISBN 0-688-02860-8 [lib. bdg.] First Mulberry Edition, 1995 ▪ ISBN 0-688-14027-0   10 9 8 7 6 5 4 3 2 1

COUNTING
WILDFLOWERS

by Bruce McMillan

A Mulberry Paperback Book
New York

Fragrant Water Lily

1 ○●●●●●●●●● ONE

Spiderwort

2

TWO

True Forget-me-not

3

THREE

Wood Lily

4

FOUR

Mullein Pink

5

FIVE

Orange Hawkweed

6

SIX

Wrinkled Rose

7

SEVEN

Chickweed

8 ○○○○○○○○●●

EIGHT

Musk Mallow

9

NINE

Sundrops

10 ⬤⬤⬤⬤⬤⬤⬤⬤⬤⬤

TEN

Maltese Cross

11

ELEVEN

Hedge Bindweed

12　TWELVE

Day Lily

13 ⬤⬤⬤⬤⬤⬤⬤⬤⬤⬤
⬤⬤⬤⬤⬤⬤⬤⬤⬤⬤

THIRTEEN

Bee Balm or Oswego Tea

14 ●●●●●●●●●●
   ●●●●●●●●●● FOURTEEN

Black Knapweed

15 FIFTEEN

Rough-fruited Cinquefoil

16

SIXTEEN

Black-eyed Susan

17

SEVENTEEN

Oxeye Daisy

18 ⭕⭕⭕⭕⭕⭕⭕⭕⭕⭕ ⭕⭕⭕⭕⭕⭕⭕⭕●● EIGHTEEN

Wild Geranium

19

NINETEEN

Common Tansy

20 ⬤⬤⬤⬤⬤⬤⬤⬤⬤⬤
⬤⬤⬤⬤⬤⬤⬤⬤⬤⬤

TWENTY

Chicory

How many?

Maiden Pink

Too many to count!

Frontis: Daisy Fleabane, *Erigeron strigosus:* Found June through October in vacant lots, fields, roadsides, along sidewalks.

1. Fragrant Water Lily, *Nymphaea odorata:* Found May through July in ponds and quiet waters.

2. Spiderwort, *Tradescantia virginiana:* Found April through June in wooded borders, thickets, meadows, and roadsides.

3. True Forget-me-not, *Myosotis scorpioides:* Found May through October along stream borders and wet places.

4. Wood Lily, *Lilium philadelphicum:* Found June through August in dry woods and thickets.

5. Mullein Pink, *Lychnis coronaria:* Found May through July in moist fields, meadows, waste places.

6. Orange Hawkweed, *Hieracium aurantiacum:* Found June through August in fields, clearings, along roadsides.

7. Wrinkled Rose, *Rosa rugosa:* Found June through September in seashore thickets, sand dunes, roadsides. *See also: Jacket.*

8. Chickweed, *Cerastium arvense:* Found February through December in lawns, vacant lots, along roadsides.

9. Musk Mallow, *Malva moschata:* Found June through October in fields, old gardens, along roadsides.

10. Sundrops, *Oenothera fruticosa:* Found June through September in fields and along roadsides.

11. Maltese Cross, *Lychnis chalcedonica:* Found June through August in thickets, open woods, and along roadsides.

12. Hedge Bindweed, *Convolvulus sepium:* Found May through September in moist places, along roadsides, vacant lots, streams.

13. Day Lily, *Hemerocallis fulva:* Found May through July along roadsides, meadows, old gardens.

14. Bee Balm or Oswego Tea, *Monarda didyma:* Found June through August in moist woods, thickets, and along streams.

15. Black Knapweed, *Centaurea nigra:* Found June through August in fields, vacant lots, waste places.

16. Rough-fruited Cinquefoil, *Potentilla recta:* Found May through August along roadsides, dry fields, city parks.

17. Black-eyed Susan, *Rudbeckia hirta:* Found June through October in fields, prairies, open woods.

18. Oxeye Daisy, *Chrysanthemum leucanthemum:* Found June through August in fields, waste places, meadows, pastures.

19. Wild Geranium, *Geranium sanguneum:* Found April through June in woods, thickets, meadows.

20. Common Tansy, *Tanacetum vulgare:* Found July through September along roadsides and edges of fields.

How many? Chicory, *Cichorium intybus:* Found June through October along roadsides, vacant lots, city parks, fields.

Too many to count. Maiden Pink, *Dianthus deltoides:* Found May through September along roadsides and in dry fields.

 Most of the flowers in this book were found in their natural habitat, though a few were discovered in the wildflower gardens of Mildred Hooper, Karen McManus, and Joan Nass. I thank each of them and the many other people who aided me with their suggestions of where and when to look for certain flowers.

All the photographs were taken in natural daylight. In most instances a reflector was used to fill in the shadows so that each flower would be easy to see and easy to count. In one instance a blue filter was used to retain the true color that exists in nature. The flowers were photographed using a Nikon F2 camera with a 55mm Micro-Nikkor f3.5 lens, sometimes with a PK-3 extension ring. All photos were taken on Kodachrome 25 or 64 transparency film and processed by Kodak.